Anonymous

Proceedings of the Massachusetts Historical Society in Respect to the Memory of William Hickling Prescott, February 1, 1859

SALZWASSER
VERLAG

Anonymous

Proceedings of the Massachusetts Historical Society in Respect to the Memory of William Hickling Prescott, February 1, 1859

Reprint of the original, first published in 1859.

1st Edition 2022 | ISBN: 978-3-37513-348-1

Verlag (Publisher): Salzwasser Verlag GmbH, Zeilweg 44, 60439 Frankfurt, Deutschland
Vertretungsberechtigt (Authorized to represent): E. Roepke, Zeilweg 44, 60439 Frankfurt, Deutschland
Druck (Print): Books on Demand GmbH, In de Tarpen 42, 22848 Norderstedt, Deutschland

Massachusetts Historical Society

IN MEMORY OF

WILLIAM HICKLING PRESCOTT.

PROCEEDINGS

OF THE

MASSACHUSETTS HISTORICAL SOCIETY

IN RESPECT TO

The Memory

OF

WILLIAM HICKLING PRESCOTT,

FEBRUARY 1, 1859.

BOSTON:

MASSACHUSETTS HISTORICAL SOCIETY.

1859.

PROCEEDINGS.

A SPECIAL MEETING of the MASSACHUSETTS HISTORICAL SOCIETY was held at their Rooms, in Tremont Street, on Tuesday evening, February 1, to express their respect for the character and services of their late eminent associate, WILLIAM HICKLING PRESCOTT, who died in Boston, on Friday, January '28, 1859.

Among other arrangements for the occasion, the beautiful bust of the lamented Historian, by Richard S. Greenough, and copies of his various Works, presented to the Society by himself, and placed upon the officers' table, were touching memorials of the loss which had been sustained.

The meeting was called to order, at half-past seven o'clock, by the President, Hon. ROBERT C. WINTHROP; who, immediately on taking the chair, addressed the members as follows: —

GENTLEMEN OF THE MASSACHUSETTS HISTORICAL SOCIETY,

You are already but too well aware of the event which has called us together. Our beautiful rooms are lighted this evening for the first time; but the shadow of an afflicting bereavement rests darkly and deeply upon our walls and upon our hearts. We are here to pay a farewell tribute to him whom we were ever most proud to welcome within our cherished circle of associates, but whose sunny smile is now left to us only as we see it yonder, in the cold though faithful outlines of art. We have come to deplore the loss of one who was endeared to us all by so many of the best gifts and graces which adorn our nature, and whose gentle and genial spirit was the charm of every company in which he mingled. We have come especially to manifest our solemn sense that one of the great Historical Lights of our country and of our age has been withdrawn from us for ever ; and to lay upon the closing grave of our departed brother some feeble but grateful acknowledgment of the honor he had reflected upon American literature, and of the renown he had acquired for the name of an American historian.

For indeed, gentlemen, we have come to this commemoration not altogether in tears. We are rather conscious at this moment of an emotion of triumph, — breaking through the sorrow which we cannot so soon shake off, — as we recall the discouragements and infirmities under which he had pressed forward so successfully to so lofty a mark, and as we remember, too, how modestly he wore the wreath which he had so gallantly won. And we thank God this night, that although he was taken away from us while many more years of happy and useful life might still have been hoped for him, and while unfinished works of the highest interest were still awaiting his daily and devoted labors, he was yet spared until he had completed so many imperishable monuments of his genius, and until he had done enough — enough — at once for his own fame and for the glory of his country. " Satis, satis est, quod vixit, vel ad ætatem vel ad gloriam."

Nor will we omit to acknowledge it as a merciful dispensation of Providence, that he was taken at last by no lingering disease, and after no protracted decline, but in the very way which those who knew him best were not unaware that he himself both expected and desired. Inheriting a name which had been associated with the noblest patriotism in one generation, and with the highest judicial wisdom in another; and having imparted a fresh lustre to that name, and secured for it a title to an even wider and more enduring remembrance, — he was permitted to approach the close of his sixty-third year in the enjoyment of as much happiness, as much respect, as much affection, as could well accompany any human career.

> " Then, with no fiery, throbbing pain,
> No cold gradations of decay,
> Death broke at once the vital chain,
> And freed his soul the nearest way."

It is not for me, gentlemen, to attempt any delineation of his character, or any description of his writings. There are those among us who have known him longer than myself, and who have established a better title to pass judgment upon his productions. Let me only say, in conclusion, that, immediately on hearing of his sudden death, permission was asked for this Society to pay the last tribute to his remains; but it was decided to be more consonant with his own unostentatious disposition, that all ceremonious obsequies should be omitted. Having followed his hearse yesterday, therefore, only as friends, we have assembled now as a Society, of which for more than twenty years he was one of the most brilliant ornaments, to give formal expression to those feelings, which, in justice either to him, to ourselves, or to the community of which he was the pride, could not longer be restrained.

It is for you, gentlemen, to propose whatever in your judgment may be appropriate for the occasion.

———

At the close of the President's remarks, Mr. G. TICKNOR rose and said:—

MR. PRESIDENT, — You have well told us why we are here at this unwonted hour. We feel the truth of every word you have uttered. The name that shone brighter than any other that was ever set on the rolls of our Society, in its distinctive attribute as a Society for the promotion of historical research, has been stricken from them, so far as such a name can be, by the hand of death. And we come to mourn together for our loss. We do not come to praise the friend and associate whom it has pleased a wise and merciful God to take away from us. His praise is beyond our reach. It extends as far as letters are valued or known. We can neither add to it nor diminish it. We come to mourn together.

I have no words of formal eulogy to offer. In this moment of sorrow, I cannot say what I would. But this I am able to say, — and it becomes the occasion that it should be said, — that to those of us who knew him from the days of his bright boyhood, down to his latest years, when he stood before the world crowned with its honors, the elements that constituted the peculiar charm of his character seemed always to be the same; that his life — his whole life — was to an extraordinary degree a happy one, governed by a pre-valent sense of duty to God and love to man; and that he has been taken from us with unimpaired faculties, and with a heart whose affections grew warmer and more tender to the last.

At the end of a life like this, although suddenly terminated, he naturally left few wishes for posthu-mous fulfilment; and the few that he did leave were of the simplest and most unpretending sort. But one was most characteristic and touching; and, as it has been accomplished, it may fitly be mentioned here. He desired that, after death, his remains might rest

for a time in the cherished room where were ga-
thered the intellectual treasures amidst which he had
found so much of the happiness of his life. His wish
was fulfilled. There he lay, — it was only yesterday,
sir, — his manly form neither wasted nor shrunk by disease; the features, which had expressed and inspired so
much love, still hardly touched by the effacing fingers
of death: there he lay, and the great lettered dead of
all ages and climes and countries seemed to look down
upon him in their earthly and passionless immortality,
and claim that his name should hereafter be imperish-
ably united with theirs. And then, when this his
wish had been fulfilled, and he was borne forth from
those doors which he had never entered except to give
happiness, but which he was never to enter again, —
then he was brought into the temple of God, where
he had been used to worship, and into a company of
the living such as the obsequies of no man of letters
have ever before assembled in this land; and there a
passionate tribute of tears and mourning was paid to
the great benefits he had conferred on the world, and
to his true and loving nature, which would have been
dearer to his heart than all the intellectual triumphs
of his life.

And now that all this is past; now that we have
laid him beside the father whom he so truly reverenced, — whom we all so reverenced, sir, — and the
mother whom he so tenderly loved, and who was loved

of all, and especially of all in sorrow and suffering, —
now what remains for us to do ?   It is little, very little.
We can express our respect, our admiration, and our
love ; we can mourn with those who were nearest and
dearest to him.   These, indeed, constitute our incum-
bent duty; and therefore, sir, I propose to you now,
even in this season of our bitter sorrow, to fulfil it,
and, as becomes such a moment, to fulfil it in the few-
est and the simplest words.

Mr. TICKNOR then read the following resolutions : —

Resolved, That, as members of the Massachusetts
Historical Society, we look back with gratitude and
pride upon the brilliant career of our late associate,
WILLIAM HICKLING PRESCOTT, who, not urged by his
social position to a life of literary toil, and discouraged
by an infirmity which seemed to forbid success, yet
chose deliberately, in his youth, the difficult path of
historical research, and, by the force of genius, of courage, and of a cheerful patience, achieved for himself,
with the full assent of Christendom, an honored place
in the company of the great masters of history in all
countries and in all ages.

Resolved, That, while we mourn the loss of one who
has thus made our country and the world his debtors,
we yet, in this moment of our sudden bereavement,
grieve rather that we miss the associate and friend
whom we loved, as he was loved of all who knew him,

2

for the beauty, the purity, and the transparent since-
rity, of his nature; for his open and warm sympathies;
and for the faithful affections, to which years and the
changes of life only added freshness and strength.

Resolved, That we request the President of this
Society to transmit these resolutions to the family of
our lamented and honored associate, expressing to
them the deep sympathy we feel in their affliction,
and commending them to the merciful God in whom
he trusted, and to the influences of that religion in
which he was wont to find consolation under trial and
suffering.

In rising to second these resolutions, JARED SPARKS, LL.D.,
offered the following remarks : —

MR. PRESIDENT, — An intimate acquaintance with
our departed associate for a long term of years, and a
friendship and affectionate esteem growing stronger
as those years advanced, have produced ties and sympathies which could not be severed without leaving a
deep impression on my mind and feelings. The
qualities of his heart, of his intellect and character,
were such as to win the steady confidence and attach-
ment of all who knew him, as many of us who are
here present have known him. But, after what has
been so well and so justly said on these topics, I shall

forbear to enlarge upon them. I rise, therefore, mainly to express my entire accordance with what has been said, and especially with the resolutions which have been offered.

I will, however, briefly touch upon those traits of his mind which qualified him for the remarkable success he attained as a historian. The highest requisites for a writer in this department of literature are a love of truth, impartiality, a discriminating judgment, and a resolute purpose to procure all the facts that can be found, enabling him to render full justice to his subject. These requisites he possessed in an eminent degree. Read his works through, and you will find the evidence of them impressed upon every page. You will find no extravagant theories, no over-wrought descriptions to disguise the faults or foibles of a favorite hero, none of the resorts of the casuist to sustain or defend a doubtful policy; in short, none of those intricate and questionable by-paths of opinion or assertion into which historians are sometimes led by their personal antipathies or partialities. Truth was his first aim, as far as he could detect it in the conflicting records of events; and his next aim was to impress this truth, in its genuine colors, upon the reader. The characters and motives of men were weighed in the scales of justice, as they appeared to him after careful research and mature thought. In all these qualities of an accomplished historian, we may safely challenge for him a comparison with any other writer.

In his unceasing efforts and extraordinary success in procuring the materials for his various historical compositions, he has certainly surpassed all other writers. Previous historians had, to some extent, made similar efforts; but I can say, with entire confidence, after my historical studies, such as they have been, that I know of no historian, in any age or language, whose researches into the materials with which he was to work have been so extensive, thorough, and profound, as those of Mr. Prescott. He was unwearied in his search after original documents, wherever they were to be found; never relying on secondary authorities, when it was possible to obtain those that were original or more to be depended upon. And it is wonderful with what success these efforts were attended, considering the sources he explored, particularly in Spain, where they had been for a long time, in a great measure, secluded from examination. But his perseverance, and, more than all, the peculiar and undisguised traits of his character, inspiring confidence in those who had this prejudice against allowing those materials to be exposed to the world, seemed to unlock every secret depository, especially after these traits had been so clearly unfolded in his first historical work. His obligations for these signal favors are freely and fully acknowledged in his prefaces; and, in the use he has made of the materials thus acquired, no one has had occasion to regret the implicit reliance that was placed on his discretion, judgment, and integrity. But, in all this, there was no ostentation or parade. He quietly pursued his course, devoting his time and thoughts to the pursuit he had chosen, and glad to gather from every quarter whatever would give more weight, character, and force to the work in which he was engaged, and thus contribute to enlighten the public, and produce the result he desired.

The theme is a broad one, Mr. President; but I will not encroach farther on the time, which may be employed with more effect by others. I will only repeat my cordial assent to what has been said by the gentlemen who have spoken, and to the sentiments expressed in the resolutions, and second those resolutions.

Rev. JAMES WALKER, D.D., President of Harvard University, then spoke as follows : —

MR. PRESIDENT, — I am the only classmate of Mr. Prescott now present. My recollections of him go back to our college-days, when he stood among us one of the youngest, one of the most joyous and light-hearted, in classic learning one of the most accomplished, without any enemies, with nothing but friends. I remember also the accident — I think it happened in our junior year — which withdrew him from us for some time, and was followed by permanent injury to his sight. Never was there a more instructive lesson on the vanity of human judgments as to what is good or evil in passing events. We all lamented it as a great calamity; yet it helped, at least, to induce that earnestness and concentration of life and pursuit which has won for him a world-wide influence and fame.

Of his subsequent career, there are many here who are better qualified to speak than I am. But I must be permitted to say one thing which was true of him from the first to the last. Of all the men whom I have known, I have never known one so little changed by the conventionalities of society, and the hard trial of success and prosperity. At college, and on the morning of the day he died, he was the same in his dispositions; the same in his outward manners; the same in his habits of thought and feeling; the same, to a remarkable degree, even in his attitudes and looks. It was because his character was a true and real character. He never aspired to become the representative of a new movement or a new idea. He was content to be himself. Hence it was, as I believe, that he suffered so little from the envies and jealousies and heart-burnings which sometimes find their way even among literary men. He was one of that happy few whom all love to hear praised.

Mr. President, I am oppressed by the occasion and the scene. The shadow of death is upon us; but it is a beautiful and accomplished life which we are called to consider, and it will do us good to ponder it well.

———

The meeting was then addressed by Hon. JOHN C. GRAY: —

MR. PRESIDENT, — If I have any right to say any thing on this occasion, it is derived from the fact, — to which my excellent friend who moved the resolutions will bear witness, — that few here can have been in closer personal contact with Mr. Prescott than I have been. It was my good fortune, forty years since, to travel with him through the most interesting portion of Europe. We all know, that, with fellow-travellers, acquaintance ripens rapidly. No man can bear better witness to his kind and genial spirit, — a spirit which had always a kind word for those to whom it could afford gratification, and which never had an ill word to utter to, or in respect to, any one. If he had the rare lot of being honored without being envied, — and who had it more ? — he reaped no more than he sowed.   He was not proud of his own distinction, and still less did he entertain any uncomfortable feelings on account of the distinction of others.   His good wishes and assistance were always at the service of those who had need of them.

I must have seen, of course, very much of the characteristics and temper of our friend, in such varieties of incident as happen to all fellow-travellers; some of them trifling in themselves, but not less apt, perhaps, to bring out uncomfortable feeling than more important emergencies which occur less frequently: and I can bear witness to his genial, kind, and cheerful spirit, — a cheerfulness that was always at the highest point, yet always sustained.   I have, of course, had much conversation with him, and heard him speak much of others, — not excepting the unfortunate young man who all but deprived him of sight, — and he never spoke of any one in other than the kindest and most Christian spirit; for, sir, he was a Christian, and in this, as in all other respects, alike free from ostentation and disguise.

I will not detain the Society longer.   They will excuse me if I say that I could not suffer this opportunity to pass — the last, perhaps, which I shall have — without offering such open testimony to his character as was prompted by my feelings, and as I was qualified to render by my personal acquaintance, if in no other respect.   I will, however, close with the narration of an incident. After Mr. Prescott had finished his first great work, so little was he inspired with a fervid ambition, or any thing like an inordinate desire for distinction, that I am told he said to his late honored father, that he had had the gratification of writing the work, and that he should place it on his shelf, and leave it for those who should come after him. He was dissuaded from so doing, and was encouraged to give it to the world; and, sir, much as we have held in remembrance the services of that honored man, his father, if what he said to his son was the means of bringing that son's works before the public, I think we shall agree that he could have rendered few services of greater moment to the community.

Mr. SPARKS again rose, and, addressing the President, said, —

If you will allow me, sir, I will detain the Society with the mention of an incident connected with the publication of Mr. Prescott's first work, — his " Ferdinand and Isabella," — which the anecdote of Mr. Gray has called to my mind. It is known that Mr. Prescott's eyesight was then so feeble, that it was difficult for him to read; and, for the purpose of carefully preparing the composition of his work, he had it printed in large type, in quarto form, so that he could read it, and correct it for the press, instead of revising it in manuscript. After it was finished, he sent me his two volumes, printed as I have described, and requested me to read them. I did so, of course, with very great pleasure and profit, and with no little surprise at the success of the writer, under his infirmity of sight, in accomplishing the work in so thorough and finished a manner. I returned the volumes; and, soon after, saw Mr. Prescott. He asked me, with a good deal of diffidence, what I thought of the book. I told him there could be but one opinion about it; that I had read the book with great delight, and thought he had written one of the most successful works of its kind that had come before the public. "But perhaps," said he, "you have read it under the bias of some degree of partiality and friendly feeling." I told him I could not say as to that; but I had been exceedingly gratified with the perusal of the book. He then asked, "Do you think it should be published?"—"To be sure," I replied: "have you not written it to be published?" He still expressed doubts, and enumerated objections. In the first place, the subject was not one likely to interest American readers: it related to Spain, and times long past. In the next place, he doubted very much whether the composition and execution of the work were of such a character as would make it attractive. His opinion was, in short, that it would not succeed.

Of course, I used what arguments I could, and told him that no impression of that sort could be entertained by any mind but his own. I left him, however, in that state of uncertainty.

Mr. Gray has explained how he was induced to publish the work at last. The anecdote is characteristic of Mr. Prescott, and illustrates his modesty, and entire freedom from self-estimation.

The meeting was next addressed by the Hon. JOSIAH QUINCY, who was admitted a member of the Society the very year in which Mr. PRESCOTT was born : —

I have been particularly requested, as one who has been a member of this Society for more than sixty years, to make some expression of my feelings on this occasion, in memory of this distinguished citizen and exemplary man ; otherwise I should not have ventured to obtrude them in the presence of so many gentlemen, who, from similarity of age, of pursuits, of taste, of genius, and long, intimate personal familiarity, are so much better qualified than I am to do justice to his singular and rare merits. As an historian, the world has already uttered all that can be said. No tribute can be paid to his worth and his talents, in this respect, which has not been already anticipated and expressed in his lifetime.

His merits were singular, and such as society does not often witness, and to which it has seldom the opportunity to do justice. He was the son of a father who, in purity of life, in elevation of sentiment, in soundness of judgment, had, among his contemporaries, no superior, and was surpassed by few, if any, in talents or legal knowledge. Had his character been of a common type, he would have sunk under the lustre of his parent's virtues, or been content to live in the enjoyment and imitation of them. But, inspired and directed by the same spirit, he saw, that, at the bar and in the senate-chamber, there was no honor to be acquired which his father had not attained; and, instinctively shunning both, he took a path in which intellectual power was less severely tested, and its rewards far more wide-spread and universal.

It is not requisite here to speak of the success and unqualified renown with which he has crowned and made immortal his memory. His merits were not only singular, but rare. Few men ever rose to such an extent and height of reputation, without, in look, language, or demeanor, indicating somewhat or somewhere a sense of the honors he had acquired. But William H. Prescott's modesty was as innate and deep-seated as his genius. The delicacy of his temperament shrunk from public notice and praise. To the merits of others, he was just and liberal; concerning his own, reserved or silent.

While cultivating the fields of literature, he practised and exemplified all the virtues, and gave new splendor and a wider sphere to the intellect he had inherited.

His life is a lesson, an incentive and example. Truth, purity, unaffected humility, combined with steady, persevering, wisely directed labor, characterized his whole course.

An accident in early life had nearly quenched his corporeal light. So much more his intellectual light seemed to burn inward, dispersing the veil of corporeal darkness, and revealing to the world a luminary casting a light on past time, in which all future time will rejoice.

The meeting was then addressed by Rev. N. L. FROTHINGHAM, D.D., Prof. C. C. FELTON, Hon. JAMES SAVAGE, and Hon. GEORGE T. CURTIS.

REMARKS OF REV. N. L. FROTHINGHAM, D.D.

MR. PRESIDENT, — Before a company where there are so many eloquent tongues, I should not have the presumption to say any thing, should have no apology for saying any thing, of our dear associate, so lately taken away from us, if it were not for the memories that travel back so far as the time when neither of us had reached the full age of manhood, for the companionship that I had the privilege of enjoying with him afterwards, and especially for the sacred relation in which I stood to him for a number of years in the ripest and most distinguished portion of his days. While he was a student in the University, I was brought into close neighborhood with him, and something like official connection. This was just before that severe calamity befell him; which one is yet hardly justified in calling a calamity, so manfully, so sweetly, so wondrously did he not only endure it, but convert it to the highest purposes of a faithful, scholarly, serviceable life. Before he published the first of those histories which have given him so proud a place in the literature, not only of his own country, but of the British and Continental world, it was my happiness to be engaged with him year after year in examining the students of the College in the modern languages, where his attendance was as freely given as if he had nothing else to do, and as if his eyes were as sound as his intellect, and where his presence was always a delight. After this, in the year 1841, he became a worshipper at the First Church, where a holier bond was formed, and where its minister might learn, from an example more shining than his lessons, the beauty of a reverent, thoughtful, dutiful Christian mind.

These are my claims, Mr. President, to say a few words; and very few are all that it will become me to say, in the midst of so much admiration and sorrow. They shall be words narrowed into one particular direction, — my conception of his private and personal worth; and this not with the slightest thought of an intent to depict his moral portrait, not to undertake to analyze in the least degree the elements of his fine nature, but simply to convey, with a touch or two, my sense of what he was, rather than of what he accomplished. Let others tell of his labors and their splendid success. Let these be set forth in all the terms of eulogy for the instruction and encouragement of youths and men, and as a just tribute to his own fame. As for me, I cannot think of these things now. Pardon me for saying such a word in a company where so many are loyal to Learning as to a sovereign mistress, and so many are enjoying the bright prizes of society; but, to my thinking, when we have just borne away our dead, literary achievement does not seem so much as it did, and the best-deserved applause has something hollow in its sound. Let me look at our valued associate only in the light of his gentle, cheerful, steadfast, noble disposition. That light came all from within. I am willing to look away at present from the broader but inferior glory.

The man was more than his books. His character was loftier than all his reputation. So simple-minded

and so great-minded; so keen in his perceptions, but
so kind in his judgments; so resolute, but so unpretending; so considerate of every one, and so tasking
of himself; so full of the truest and warmest affections;
so merry in his temper, without overleaping a single
due bound; such spirit, but such equanimity; so much
thoughtfulness, without the least cast of sickliness;
doing good as by the instinct of spontaneous activity,
and doing labor without a wrinkle or a strain; un-
swerving in his integrity, and with the nicest sense of
honor; whom no disadvantage could dishearten, no
prosperity corrupt, no honors and plaudits elate or
alter one whit; modest, as if he had never done any
thing; retaining through life all the artlessness of the
highest wisdom; with a liberal heart and an open
hand; the ingenuousness of youth flashing to the
last from his frank face; walking in sympathy with
his fellows, and humbly before God. Ah! Mr. President, we ought to make some allowance for those
who, born with a less genial and upward nature, of a
more stubborn material or ruder shape, with fewer
of those native endowments and appetences which
come direct from the Father of spirits, are unable to
perform so much.

I will do no more than repeat a single anecdote, so
characteristic of our lamented friend, that, simple as it
is, it will bear to be recorded as a representative fact.
His mother — and, truly, who was ever descended from

a nobler parentage on both sides than he?—his mother, as she sat with me one day in my study, said, "This is the very room where William was shut up for so many months in utter darkness. , In all that trying season, when so much had to be endured, and our hearts were ready to fail us for fear, I never in a single instance groped my way across the apartment to take my place at his side, that he did not salute me with some hearty expression of good cheer,—not in a single instance; as if we were the patients, and it was his place to comfort us." No word of complaint through all that dismal period; no sigh of impatience or regret. He was not content even with the perfect silence of an unrepining will; but he must sing in that imprisonment and night. Is this *not* a representative example? We cannot be surprised at any thing that followed after this. Was not this the man to win crowns of laurel and oak, and to wear them as if they were the natural growth of his hair?

And now that he has been just so long gone that the wound of his loss is fresh, and the grief sore, and yet there has been time for the shock to subside, and reflection to claim its healing office, I think we must feel it to be good for him and us that he was taken away by a noiseless appointment and a swift angel, just as it was,—just as it was; that the second touch of his malady was so absolute:—

"No pale gradations quenched his ray,
No twilight mists."

4

" Felix, Agricola, non vitæ tantùm claritate, sed etiam opportunitate mortis." He was taken in the midst of his honorable toils, his high faculties, his bright name, his full tides of intellect and love, his troops and armies of admiring regards, on the verge of the grand climacteric of his well-used years. No one will take up and carry on his unfinished tasks. Who can? who need? We can bear that deprivation. But we do not know how we should have borne the slow crumbling of so rare a mansion; the crippling of so sweet an energy; the clouding over, deeper and deeper, of that clear intellect; the fitful freezing and thawing, stopping and flowing, of the currents of the diviner life. We will hide our eyes from that terrible peril. We will give thanks that he was taken, though snatched, from so dreary an evil. All is well with him now. He is emancipated, and not exposed or bound.

> " These shall swim after death, with their choice deeds
> Shining on their white shoulders."

REMARKS OF PROF. C. C. FELTON.

MR. PRESIDENT, — I thank you for the opportunity you allow me to add my voice to the voices of those who have given utterance here to the universal grief for this late public and private bereavement. Sir, I cannot say one word which will add to the fame of

William H. Prescott; but hereafter it will be a consolation to me, through all my life, that I had the privilege of mingling my tears with the tears of those who were nearest to him through the longest period of his life, under these circumstances, in this venerable presence of the living, and the awful presence of the great departed, whose pictured and marble forms and printed works surround us. No one knew Mr. Prescott but to love him. It was not my privilege to know him in his early years; but I have been an acquaintance, I hope I may say a friend, certainly a lover, of his, during the greater portion of my own life; and I think I may say with truth, that no death in this or any other community would touch with affliction more hearts than have been and will be saddened by his death.

Not only those (and there are thousands) who knew him personally, but those who knew him only in the printed page, — those who knew him in those beautiful works, — seemed to know the loveliness of his character, and to feel for their author all the tenderness of personal affection. It is a saying, that " the style is the man; " and of no great author in the literature of the world is that saying more true than of him whose loss we mourn. For in the transparent simplicity and undimmed beauty and candor of his style were read the endearing qualities of his soul; so that his personal friends are found wherever litera-

ture is known, and the love for him is co-extensive
with the world of letters, — not limited to those who
speak our Anglo-Saxon mother-language, to the literature of which he has contributed such splendid
works, but co-extensive with the civilized languages
of the human race.

Mr. President, on the 5th of last May, — the day
of my embarkation for Europe, — I called at Mr.
Prescott's house, knowing how earnest and affectionate would be the inquiries made with regard to him
by those friends of his whom I should chance to meet
abroad, and anxious to give to them the last best news
I could upon the state of his health. And so, indeed,
it was. No sooner had I touched my foot upon the
English shores, than questions with regard to his condition were addressed to me by numerous English
friends; and I happened to meet some of those who
had known him best and most affectionately in this
country and in Europe. It was a satisfaction to me,
that I had it in my power to give them the latest
news on a subject which seemed to interest the heart
of the whole literary world.

Mr. President, scholars everywhere will feel this
bereavement; literary and scientific societies will
notice it by commemorative rites. What a cloud will
come over that fair and romantic land, whose history
and literature he has done so much to adorn! In
Germany, where his profound learning and his vast

acquirements in the department of history were thoroughly appreciated, and where his name is one of the greatest, — there, too, will his loss be deeply felt. In beautiful and unfortunate Italy, of whose literature he had early felt the charm, and over whose storied sites he had wandered in his youth, the name of Prescott has become a classic name. Ay, sir, more than that. In the lovely land where historical composition had its origin, — in the land of Hellas, redeemed again to freedom, letters, and art, — even there the name of Prescott has become a classic name. Sir, it was only last July that I had the pleasure of looking upon the works of our distinguished countryman, and of his lifelong friend who introduced these resolutions, standing side by side, in the University of Athens, with those of the illustrious native masters.

Sir, this sad news will speed over the earth and sea on the wings of the lightning. With the loveliness of returning spring, the announcement will be heard, even to the shores of Greece, that a great and pure light has been withdrawn from the Western World. It will come upon the festive rites of that most ancient Oriental church, that has survived so many ages of woe; and, under the matchless glories of the sky of Attica, a sense of bereavement and a wail of sorrow will mingle with the festivities and Christian welcomes of that joyous season. Be assured, sir, that, before the summer comes, eloquent eulogies upon the character and works of our departed countryman will be pronounced before crowded audiences of Hellenic youth, in the language of Thucydides and Xenophon, in that same illustrious Athens where those great ancients lived whose renown has made her name immortal.

Sir, this death of Mr. Prescott, which has fallen with such appalling suddenness upon us, struck me in a peculiar manner. It so happened, that, owing to a multiplicity of occupations since my return from Europe, I had not seen my friend, as I will venture to call him: and last Saturday, having a leisure day, I said to myself, " I will go early to town ; and the first thing I do shall be to call on Mr. Prescott, and tell him something of what his friends abroad have said to me." Passing from my own house to the railroad, I stepped over to the Post Office, and took my morning papers; and, on opening one of them, the first words that struck my astonished eyes were those announcing the death of William Hickling Prescott !

Sir, I deplore, and shall deplore to my dying day, that I have not seen and conversed with Mr. Prescott for some months past; that, after parting with him in May, I met him only at the gate of the tomb to say a last farewell : but I shall console myself with the thought, that I have had the opportunity of adding my feeble voice to the earnest and eloquent testimonials to his great name and his lovely character on this occasion. One of those great writers and teachers of the historic art to whom I have alluded — Thucydides — speaks of " that simplicity in which nobleness of nature most largely shares," as the highest style of man; and surely to no man, before or since the days of the profound historian of the Peloponnesian war, do those words apply with more pertinency and force than to the character of Prescott. And, as he lived, so he died.

Great as the shock was, sad as this bereavement is, bitter as are our feelings in the first moments of our loss, we must all acknowledge that he accomplished a noble and brilliant life ; and, though he left works unfinished, whenever that great summons came, it would find him so employed, that works would still be left unfinished. For, Mr. President, it is not the lot of man to finish his tasks here below : that can only be done in the world above. But, sir, as my reverend friend has said, he was called away in the midst of happiness, as if by an angelic messenger. The summons came in a moment. It found him enjoying the light of the domestic hearth ; and, in an instant, his spirit was translated into the light of Eternal Love. That, Mr. President, was the euthanasia of our friend and associate.

REMARKS OF HON. JAMES SAVAGE.

MR. PRESIDENT, — Enough has been said here, by
those who enjoyed the acquaintance of Mr. Prescott,
to afford to others a just estimate of his character;
for few could have acquaintance with him that was
not an intimate one. He was transparent in such
uncommon degree, that, in a short time, whoever
was acquainted with him might become conversant
with his character. Sir, it does not always happen,
— but I thank Heaven the instances are not rare, —
in which from a glorious father is derived a son with
strong resemblance. Here have been three genera-
tions of this stock claiming highest regard from the
people of Massachusetts, and for very diverse qualities.
He who commanded on Bunker Hill is known only,
but universally, for his intrepidity. Brave to a degree
beyond what belongs to the general spirit of soldiery,
having labored all night in throwing up the works on
that commanding spot; entitled, as his commander
thought, to defend them through the day, — yet was he
not a braver man than his son William, distinguished
for widely different public service. The stainless honor
of Judge Prescott needed not to be shown in deadly
combat; but whoever weighed his merit felt that he
would have sustained at every hazard, even of instant
death, the calm assertion of duty in vindication of the
rights of his fellow-men.

After the full and appropriate estimate of the private virtues and literary reputation, the endowments and acquisitions, of our late associate, I would ask, confidently, for a review of his characteristic and hereditary distinction, — of unusual bravery in his pursuits. What is the first requisite the Muse of History demands of her admirers? The truth, in every respect; the truth, in spite of all opposition; the truth with mildness, and with the affection and dignity that accompanied every word that Mr. Prescott ever said on paper or in the utterance of speech. Sir, he, more than any other man, I think, of my acquaintance, — and I refer to the delightful illustrations of his classmate, and to the more delightful remarks which came from his religious instructor; I refer to what is known by his most intimate friends, — he was a man who could stand up before the universe, and challenge any aspersion. There never was a man who spoke ill of him. He eminently is exposed to the woe that, it is said, belongs to him " of whom all men speak well."

Mr. President, I ought not to have said half as much as I have; and yet, though it is late, I did not dare to sit still any longer, for fear that a sufficiently impressive intonation should not be given to the highest merit of that man's character. It is not his distinction attained in letters. It is not that the world round, where the English language is read, and the various languages into which his works have been translated, — the French, the German, the Spanish, and the Italian, — there is not remaining on this earth a man of higher literary merit; I will not say distinction. There may be one or another superior by metaphysical acquisition, by mathematical endowments, or diffusing good throughout the world; but my departed friend never knew the temptation of adopting an equivocal expression, or even the metaphysical refinement that conceals one. No man could ever charge him with it. He was solely seeking for Truth in the best recesses where Truth is found; and he has done more than any other living man to bring her forth in her full majesty. Greater difficulties no writer encountered, and none ever triumphed over them more fully. I would, sir, refer more particularly to what was so admirably touched upon by his classmate and by his religious instructor; and I have looked also for many years upon the very same, — happiness I call it; and happiness it will be, when we think of it, — upon his happiness while suffering from what is commonly called an accident, — a casualty we will call it (but if there be a Providence in any thing, not to govern nations, not to regulate this sidereal system only, but applying to each individual, then that misfortune, as it seems, was the greatest good); upon his happiness, when he was submitted to that awful darkness to which no ray of light was permitted. His father and his mother and his sister may well have hoped that it should be well with William, even under such a disaster. But he himself, for now near thirty years, has manifested to all the world the blessing which our great religious poet has illustrated for his own case, in the prayer, —

> "So much the rather thou, Celestial Light!
> Shine inward, and the mind through all her powers
> Irradiate."

REMARKS OF HON. GEORGE T. CURTIS.

MR. PRESIDENT, — Standing less near, in age and in association, to him whom this whole community now mourns, than those who have addressed you, I yet desire to lay an humble tribute of admiration upon his tomb; feeling how true it is, that we have now lost one, who, in the language of these resolutions, will be admitted everywhere to be entitled to the name and the rank of a great historian; and who, in his relation to us, added to this title that of a near and dear friend.

I have said, sir, that we have now lost him. I should correct that expression. We have, indeed, lost the daily greeting, the friendly grasp, the genial smile, — all that was the earthly presence of this illustrious writer and beloved friend. All unfinished, too, — as when some great sculptor is stricken down with the chisel in his hand, — lies the last of those splendid monuments which his genius led him to undertake for the delight and instruction of mankind. Yet how much remains! That reputation, co-extensive with Christendom, which has brought so much honor upon our country, upon our city, and upon us; that example of victory over personal infirmities, and of victory over the allurements of a social position exempt from the necessity of toil, — an example which has carried, and is yet to carry, consolation and encouragement to the struggling scholar in all lands, — which appeals, and is yet to appeal, so powerfully to the wealthy youth of our own country; that beautiful character, which has caused a whole community to feel as if touched by a personal loss, and to pour their tears upon his grave, as for one who was their own; those works, which are to exist so long as any vestiges of our civilization remain, side by side with the imperishable writings of the chief historians of all ages, — these are *not* lost, because they are of the fruits, for the production of which our immortal nature was placed in this mortal sphere.

Mr. President, if I had felt that it was the sole purpose of these proceedings to express the grief of personal affection, I should not have ventured to address you; for, although I have for many years

been honored by the personal regard of the late Mr.
Prescott, what belongs to the duties of friendship has
come, and will doubtless again come, from others.
But to me, sir, an humble amateur in that noble art
in which our lamented friend was so distinguished,
this occasion has — I would not say a higher, for
what can be higher or holier than the last rites of
love ? — to me this occasion has a further interest.   It
seems to me to call, not for vindication, not for de-
fence, not for challenge ; but for the briefest and most
simple statement of the value and dignity of the labors
of our deceased friend, as they are expressed in the
first of the resolutions on your table.

The pursuit to which Mr. Prescott devoted his life
is universally felt, among the cultivated part of mankind, to be one of the highest forms of intellectual
labor; yet it is probable that even educated men do
not always fully appreciate the qualities, the powers,
and the tasks of a truly great historian.   The general
public can, of course, only take the finished work of
art as it comes, all compact in its exceeding beauty
and fitness, from the hands of the great master, and
admire and learn, and be grateful.   Of that research,
which must leave no fact, however minute, untried ;
of that judicial temper, which must yield to no prejudice ; of that large and catholic sympathy with
human progress, without which there can be no permanent success ; of that courage which declares the

truth, though it be unwelcome; of that power to weigh events, to detect causes, to make the wide deductions on which the judgment of the future is to rest for its opinions of the past; and of that final process which fixes forever, in a work of high art, the teachings of Providence as displayed in the moral world, — of all these great requirements and these varied accomplishments we see little, or think little, as we pass, delighted and improved, over the printed page.

Such a master of his art was he whom we mourn. The subjects which he chose for the exercise of his noble powers were in those departments of history, in which the lives of princes, the intrigues of courts, the characters and actions of individuals, and the movements of armies, necessarily occupy a very prominent place. This is no time, nor is this the occasion, nor is he who now speaks of him the person, to show how successfully his works refute that theory, which we sometimes hear uttered as a complaint, that in history, as it has hitherto been written, man is neglected, and governments are made all in all. I am sure, that, when the ultimate judgment of his contemporaries or of posterity shall be pronounced, the works of Prescott will not lose their place in the estimation of the world through the operation of any sound canon of criticism that may now exist, or that may be called into existence hereafter. I found this expectation upon two positions, — first, that it is in the order of Providence that the characters, the acts, and lives of individuals shall have a vast influence on the welfare, the condition, and the progress of society; and, secondly, that this great writer has perceived, with as clear a vision and as just a discrimination as have been given to the foremost masters in this difficult art, how to unite the exhibition of that influence with the display of those general causes and those uniform laws which control even the despotism of princes, and subject the arbitrary will of man to the overruling purposes of God.

But let me turn, sir, from these anticipations of the future, to dwell for a moment upon that present fame which he enjoyed in such a bountiful harvest. It is now nearly nine years, since, on a visit abroad, I met Mr. Prescott in London, and witnessed that remarkable ovation which he there received. I suppose that such a reception has not been accorded in modern England to any other merely literary and private man of any country. I attributed it at the time, in part, to the fact that he was an American, and that he had written in the language which is their and our common inheritance. Partly also, no doubt, it was due to the charm of his manners and conversation, and to the frank and genial facility with which he could adapt himself to all companies. The peculiar sympathy and admiration, too, which were excited by the extraordinary difficulties under which his works had been produced, quickened the interest that was taken in the author.

But I could not fail to be struck with the character and extent of his reputation, for which none of these things would account.   I was there before him; and, when his purpose to make this visit was known, it is no exaggeration to say, that, in all ranks and all forms of society in which intelligent men and women were found, there was evident a sensation of anticipated pleasure, a delighted expectation of curiosity and interest, which no countryman of his could witness without pride.   What followed after his arrival, you all know.   Public and private honors, the homage of the head and the homage of the heart, were showered upon him by all ranks.   What followed on his return to that home and that society which he loved above all human associations, you know equally well.

Neither the flatteries of the great, the fascinations of that brilliant society in which he was an honored guest, nor any single circumstance of his personal success, changed the simplicity of his character, or imparted to it one tinge of arrogance.   My opportunities to observe the complexion of his feelings were ample; for I returned in the same ship with him, and had with him many hours of the freest intercourse during every day of the voyage: and I declare here this night, as a testimony due to the manliness, the sweetness, and the nobleness of his nature, that I have never seen the man on whom great fame and extraordinary social success had a less disturbing effect than they had on him. That he had a solid and just satisfaction in all that was manifested towards him, I could perceive; but, if we would estimate him rightly, we must remember that few men could have passed through those scenes without bringing away more traces of that which intoxicates, than of that which strengthens and enlarges, the soul. He brought nothing which our most jealous love could have wished him to escape. On the day when we landed, and he returned into the bosom of his family, into the quiet seclusion of his library, and his accustomed walk of life, he was the same man as when he went forth to meet the delighted homage of Europe. Place, oh! place *this* token of him before the eyes of all our countrymen.

He is gone! If it had pleased Almighty God to have permitted us one word of farewell, we should doubtless have heard him call to us, as we can now only hail his departed spirit, —

> " Say not ' Good-night!'
> But, in another clime, bid me ' Good-morning!' "

The resolutions which had been offered by Mr. TICKNOR were then unanimously adopted; the members rising when the question was taken.

The President then said : —

GENTLEMEN, — We are deprived this evening of the presence of more than one of those whom we are always delighted to have with us. My friend Mr. Everett is absent from home, and will not return for ten or twelve days. I know he will deeply regret having lost the opportunity of uniting in this commemoration of one of his most cherished friends.

I have the following notes before me, — the first being from our worthy and respected Vice-President, the Hon. DAVID SEARS : —

BEACON STREET, Feb. 1, 1859.

MY DEAR MR. WINTHROP, — I regret that a severe cold confines me to my room, and will prevent my assisting at the meeting of the Historical Society called for this evening to pay a last tribute of respect to our excellent friend and associate, William H. Prescott.

I was not able to attend his funeral yesterday, and I am not able to attend our meeting to-day. I feel the deprivation sensibly; and, in spite of my judgment, it is accompanied by a sort of consciousness that I am not doing for him what I am sure he would readily have done for me.

My acquaintance with Mr. Prescott dates back nearly half a century; for, even in his boyhood, he was often the bearer of important papers between his father and myself.

His literary fame is spread through the civilized world; but his endearing social qualities are known only to those who enjoyed his intimacy. The world will lament the historian and the scholar: his associates alone can estimate the companion and the man. But both will readily class him in the highest rank as scholar, gentleman, and friend.

Very faithfully yours,

DAVID SEARS.

Hon. ROBERT C. WINTHROP,
    President Mass. Historical Society.

BOSTON, Feb. 1, 1859.

DEAR SIR, — I regret extremely that the state of my health will not allow me to attend the special meeting to-night, to be held in "respect to the memory of our late distinguished associate," Mr. Prescott.

I should regret still more to be thought insensible to his great fame and merit, or to doubt his title to any tribute which the Society, this city, and the world of letters, may unite to bestow upon him.

Please to consider me as personally with you, and warmly approving of all you shall do or say in memory of him.

I am, sir, your obedient servant,

RUFUS CHOATE.

Rev. CHANDLER ROBBINS, D.D.,
    Recording Secretary of the Historical Society.

REMARKS OF HON. EDWARD EVERETT,

MADE AT A STATED MONTHLY MEETING OF THE SOCIETY,

Thursday, 10th of February, 1859.

———

Mr. President, — At the special meeting of the
Society, held on the 1st instant, to take becoming notice
of the death of our honored and lamented associate,
Mr. Prescott, you kindly apologized, with your usual
thoughtfulness, for my necessary absence. I was in
the State of New Jersey that day, under a public en-
gagement; and it was only by the aid of the telegraph
that I received the notice of the meeting. You will
readily believe that I regretted most deeply my in-
ability to join you in the last tribute of respect to the
memory of our friend, paid with so much feeling and
pathetic eloquence, on behalf of the Massachusetts
Historical Society, by our worthy associates who took
part in that day's proceedings. If I now ask permission to add a few words to what was so appropriately
and touchingly said by them, it is not that the departed
needs my poor testimony; not that the Society needs
my aid in doing honor to his beloved name; but that
I myself, the friend of more than forty years' standing,
may not seem wanting on an occasion of such affecting
interest.

Being about to leave home on Monday, the 24th of January, on a visit to Philadelphia, and taking my accustomed walk in the middle of the day on the Saturday preceding, I met our late lamented and beloved associate.   He seemed to me as well as at any time the past twelvemonth; but my son, who was with me, thought his countenance somewhat changed.   On the following Friday, the telegraph transmitted the news of his death to Philadelphia; where, I think I can truly say, it was mourned as deeply and sincerely as anywhere in Boston, out of the circle of immediate relatives and friends.   They felt his death as a loss, not of any one place, but of the whole country.   And this feeling I found universally prevalent in a somewhat extensive circuit since made in New Jersey; in New York, where a most distinguished brother historian (Mr. Bancroft) gave utterance, in language the most appropriate and impressive, to the unaffected sorrow of the community; and in the neighboring city of Brooklyn, which I have since visited.   Everywhere, Mr. President, those tributes of respect and affection which have been paid to our dear friend by his neighbors, associates, and immediate fellow-citizens, have found a ready response throughout the country, as they will throughout the civilized world.

I can add nothing to what has been already said in the general contemplation of his eminence as an author, his worth as a man, his geniality as a companion, his fidelity as a friend; his severe trials, his heroic exertions, his glorious success. But I have thought it might be in my power to say a few words not unacceptably of the rapidity and the extent to which his reputation was established abroad, and the prompt and generous recognition of his ability in Europe. The "History of Ferdinand and Isabella" was published at the close of 1837 or the beginning of 1838; and, on my arrival in Europe in the summer of 1840, I found it extensively known and duly appreciated. Mr. Prescott, following down the stream of Spanish history, had already conceived the project of writing, at some future period, the history of Philip II., after he should have narrated, in works to be prepared in the interval, the magnificent episodes of the "Conquest of Mexico and Peru." I remonstrated with him for passing over the reign of the Emperor Charles V.; urging upon him, that the materials which had become accessible since Robertson's time, especially the archives of Simancas (the want of access to which was so much deplored by that author), would enable him to treat that period to as good advantage as that of Ferdinand and Isabella, or Philip. But he modestly persisted in thinking that the reign of Charles V. was exhausted by Robertson. The supplementary chapter with which he has enriched the edition of Robertson's work, published under his supervision a few years since, is a sufficient proof that it would have been in his power to construct an original history of the reign of Charles V., which would have fully equalled in interest any that has been produced by him.

He requested me to make some preliminary inquiries at Paris in reference to materials for Philip II.; especially to obtain information as to the portion of the archives of Simancas which had been carried in the time of Napoleon to Paris, and were still detained there. No difficulty attended a thorough exploration of the rich materials in the royal library; but the papers from Simancas were guarded with greater care in the " Archives of the Kingdom." The whole of that celebrated national collection had been transported to Paris in the time of Napoleon; and after his downfall, and in the general restoration, those portions of the archives which purported to relate to the history of France were, in spite of the urgent and oft-repeated reclamations of the Spanish government, retained in Paris. It was natural, under these circumstances, that they should be watched with some jealousy: but the name of Mr. Prescott was a key which unlocked the depository; and by the kindness of M. Mignet, who had himself examined them with diligence, they were fully thrown open to my inspection on his behalf.

The same result followed a similar application at Florence the following year. Not only were the pri-

vate collections of the Marquis Gino Capponi and the
Count Guicciardini (the lineal descendant of the historian) thrown open to the use of Mr. Prescott, but,
after tedious hesitations and delays on the part of
subordinate officials, a peremptory order was at length
issued by Prince Corsini, with the consent of the
Grand Duke of Tuscany, that I should be allowed to
explore the Medicean Archives (Archivio Mediceo),
and mark for transcription whatever I thought would
be useful for Mr. Prescott. When I add that this
magnificent collection of eighty thousand volumes
(since greatly augmented, as I learn from my friend
Mr. Ticknor, by bringing together all the provincial
archives of every part of the Grand Duchy), the examination of which was rendered easy by a copious
index, contained the correspondence of the Tuscan
minister at Madrid, during the entire reign of Philip
II., it will be readily conceived how rich were the
materials for the history of that period. Nothing
that I marked for transcription was refused. It was
sufficient that I thought it would be useful to Mr.
Prescott; and among the portions of the correspondence which I was able in this way to procure for him
were the semi-weekly communications of the Tuscan
minister on the arrest, imprisonment, and death of
Don Carlos. That papers so delicate — guarded
with such jealousy for three centuries — should have
been fully thrown open by a Catholic sovereign to an

American Protestant writer, bears witness at once to the liberality of the Grand Duke, and the European reputation of our lamented friend.

Nor was his fame less promptly and substantially established in England. Calling one day on the venerable Mr. Thomas Grenville, whom I found in his library (the second in size and value of the private libraries of England), reading Xenophon's " Anabasis " in the original, I made some passing remark on the beauty of that work. " Here," said he, holding up a volume of " Ferdinand and Isabella," " is one far superior." With the exception of the Nestor of our literature (Mr. Irving), no American writer appeared to me so widely known or so highly esteemed in England as Mr. Prescott; and, when he visited that country a few years later, the honors paid to him by all the cultivated classes of society, from the throne downward, were such as are seldom offered to the most distinguished visitant.

This is not the time nor the place for a critical disquisition on the merits of our lamented associate as a writer of history; nor am I prepared — arrived but last evening from an arduous journey, filled up with engagements which have left me no moment of leisure — to undertake the task. It would, moreover, be a work of supererogation. The public mind has passed judgment on his merits, in a manner to need no confirmation and to fear no contradiction. When, in

7

after-times, the history of our American literature shall be written, it will be told with admiration, how, in the front rank of a school of contemporary historical writers flourishing in the United States in the second quarter of the nineteenth century, more numerous and not less distinguished than those of any other country, a young man, who was not only born to affluence and exposed to all its seductions, but who seemed forced into inaction by the cruel accident of his youth, devoted himself to that branch of literary effort which seems most to require the eyesight of the student, and composed a series of historical works not less remarkable for their minute and accurate learning, than their beauty of style, calm philosophy, acute delineation of character, and sound good sense. No name more brilliant than his will descend to posterity on the roll of American authors.

But it will not be in this Association alone that he will be honored in after-times. So long as in ages far distant, and not only in countries now refined and polished, but in those not yet brought into the domain of civilization, the remarkable epoch which he has described shall attract the attention of men; so long as the consolidation of the Spanish monarchy and the expulsion of the Moors, the mighty theme of the discovery of America, the sorrowful glories of Columbus, the mail-clad forms of Cortez and Pizarro and the other grim *conquistadores*, trampling new-found em-

pires under the hoofs of their cavalry, shall be subjects
of literary interest; so long as the blood shall curdle
at the cruelties of Alva, and the fierce struggles of the
Moslem in the East, — so long will the writings of our
friend be read. With respect to some of them, time,
in all human probability, will add nothing to his
materials. It was said the other day by our respected
associate, President Sparks (a competent authority),
that no historian, ancient or modern, exceeded Mr.
Prescott in the depth and accuracy of his researches.
He has driven his artesian criticism through wretched
modern compilations, and the trashy exaggerations of
intervening commentators, down to the original contemporary witnesses; and the sparkling waters of
truth have gushed up from the living rock. In the
details of his narrative, farther light may be obtained
from sources not yet accessible. The first letter of
Cortez may be brought to light; the hieroglyphics
of Palenque may be deciphered: but the history of
the Spanish empire, during the period for which he
has treated it, will be read by posterity for general
information, not in the ancient Spanish authors, not
in black-letter chronicles, but in the volumes of Prescott.

Finally, sir, among the masters of historical writing
— the few great names of ancient and modern renown
in this department — our lamented friend and associate has passed to a place among the most honored

and distinguished. Whenever this branch of polite literature shall be treated of by some future Bacon, and the names of those shall be repeated, who have possessed in the highest degree that rare skill by which the traces of a great plan in the fortunes of mankind are explored, and the living body of a nation is dissected by the keen edge of truth, and guilty kings and guilty races summoned to the bar of justice, and the footsteps of God pointed out along the pathways of time, his name will be mentioned with the immortal trios of Greece and of Rome, and the few who in the modern languages stand out the rivals of their fame.

No one can speak of our dear departed friend without recollecting the infirmity under which he labored the greater part of his days, and with which Providence, in his case, applied the solemn law of compensation, by which the blessings of life are enjoyed, and endowments balanced by sorrows. To some it is given to ascend the heights of fame through the narrow and cheerless path of penury. Others toil patiently on beneath a load of domestic care and bereavement, — the loss of the dutiful, the hopeful, and the beloved. For him that dares to intrude on public life (as our friend never did), ferocious detraction stands ready to fly at his throat, and petty malice to yelp at his heels. Our friend achieved the miracle of his unexampled success under the pri-

vation — at times the total privation — of the dearest
of the senses, —that through which the spirit of man
is wedded to the lovely forms of the visible universe.
At intervals, for some years before he commenced his
historical labors, for him, as for the kindred genius by
whose example he tells us he took courage, —

> " Seasons returned; but not for him returned
> Day, or the sweet approach of even or morn,
> Or sight of vernal bloom, or summer's rose,
> Or flocks, or herds, or human face divine."

But he went from his darkened chamber and his
couch of pain to his noble work, as a strong man
rejoicing to run a race. A kind Providence at intervals raised the veil from his eyes, and his sweet
resignation and heroic fortitude turned his trials into
a blessing. His impaired sight gave him concentrated
mental vision: and so he lived his great day, illustrious without an enemy, successful without an envier;
wrought out his four historical epics to the admiration
of the age; and passed away at the grand climacteric,
not of years alone, but of love and fame.

> " Τὸν πέρι Μοῦσ' ἐφίλησε, δίδου δ' ἀγαθόν τε κακόν τε·
> Ὀφθαλμῶν μὲν ἄμερσε, δίδου δ' ἡδεῖαν ἀοιδήν."